Nestor *the* Monster

Nestor *the* Monster

by

Nigel Tranter

B&W PUBLISHING • EDINBURGH

B&W PUBLISHING • 7 SCIENNES • EDINBURGH • 031-667 6679

The characters in this book are entirely imaginary and
have no relation to any living person

First published by Brockhampton Press Ltd
This edition published 1992 by B&W Publishing
Edinburgh
ISBN 0 9515151 8 7

British Library Cataloguing in Publication Data:
A catalogue record for this book is available from
the British Library

Cover design by *Harry Palmer* **Design** *Consultants*

Cover illustration by Gaynor Shephard

Printed by Billings of Worcester

Contents

1
Invitation to Adventure

'PLEASE, Daddy, *may* I go?' Fiona pleaded. 'I'd like to, very much. I know I've had one holiday already this year. But - well, there would be only my fare to pay. And I've got a little saved up.'

'H'rrr'mmm,' the Reverend Mr MacBride said loudly, dragging his eyes from his book. 'We can't all do just everything that we should like to do, my dear. Just as well, no doubt. I... ah... umm.'

'I know that, Daddy, but there's no harm in doing what we want to do *occasionally*, is there? I mean, maybe even twice in one year?'

Her father frowned. 'Fiona, that is verging on hypocrisy,' he said, trying hard to sound stern - which was a little difficult, for he was not really a stern sort of man. 'And hypocrisy is a sin.'

'Yes, Daddy,' his daughter agreed dutifully, and added, 'I could go and see Aunt Edith in Inverness.'

The Reverend Mr MacBride almost choked.

'That, child, is worse!' he spluttered. 'When, before this, have you ever shown the least desire to visit your Aunt Edith, I'd like to know?'

'Well, better late than never, perhaps,' his red-headed only child suggested, traitorously using one of the minister's own favourite sayings against him. 'She's getting old, after all. You don't want me not to call on Aunt Edith, Daddy?'

'H'rrr'mmm,' Mr MacBride coughed again. 'Of course not. I mean, not at all. That's not the point. Anyway, this place, this Ardroy, may not be anywhere near Inverness. Just because it's in Inverness-shire...'

'It is, Daddy. I've looked it up. It's only about fifteen miles away.' She paused, and then spoke very casually indeed. 'Actually it's quite near Loch Ness.'

'Fifteen miles is quite a distance.... Loch Ness, did you say?'

Fiona nodded warily, pink tongue moistening her lip. 'Yes. Somewhere there.'

'M'mmm,' her father murmured, pinching his chin. 'You might just possibly see the Loch Ness Monster.'

It was Fiona's turn almost to choke. Her father had not sounded sarcastic. She did not risk saying anything just then.

'It is in the Castle Urquhart and Drumnadrochit area that the creature is usually seen, isn't it?' Mr

MacBride went on. 'Is this place, this Ardroy where Ken is, anywhere near there?'

'Just - just across the loch,' Fiona got out.

'Indeed. Interesting. Very.' Mr MacBride nodded. 'You might have quite a good chance of a view of it then.'

Fiona swallowed. 'You mean... you really believe in the Monster, Daddy? That it's not just a story?'

'Tut, girl, of course I do! Anybody with a spark of intelligence does. After all, it's a well-known fact that in the old days monsters and water-kelpies and strange creatures dwelt in half the lochs of Scotland. No historian can doubt it. The legends and folk-tales of the Highlands are full of them. It is certain that they were not all invented for the benefit of future tourists! Besides, this one has been seen by many reliable people: policemen, gamekeepers, and even a parish minister.'

Fiona almost thrust Ken's letter under her father's nose, but some unusual streak of caution held her back. 'Then can I go, Daddy?' she demanded.

'Well... ummm... er, not so fast, young lady. After all, I don't suppose you'd give a single thought to looking for the creature once you got there. If I know you and young Ken Rutherford, you'd be off all the time on some exceedingly wild goose chase of your own! If it isn't dredging up Spanish galleons and hunting salmon poachers, it's getting lost in the

Cheviots and chasing sheep-stealers! I daren't trust the pair of you out of my sight!'

'But, Daddy, if I promised, word of honour, to spend a lot of my time, quite a lot, doing nothing but watching the loch for the Monster, would you say I could go?'

'Well, maybe, if I had a firm promise...'

'It's yours, Daddy. Firm as... as reinforced concrete!' Jumping up, Fiona planted a kiss on her father's bald spot, and raced away upstairs. She was careful to take her letter with her.

Up in her own room, Fiona read through Ken's letter again. It was addressed from Ardroy Lodge Hotel, Ardroy, Inverness-shire, headed *Secret and Confidential*, and read as follows:

Dear Fiona,

You may be surprised to get a letter from me from up here - to get one at all, maybe, for I am not much of a letter-writer. But this is rather special. I've had a great job getting my father to take his fishing holiday up here this year. He seemed to want to go almost anywhere except Loch Ness-side. Mummy didn't care much where she went, but Daddy was awfully difficult. However, I managed it, for there's a good stretch of salmon river attached to this hotel - it's a converted shooting-lodge, you see. So everything's okay.

It's like this, Fiona. 'The News Dispatch' is

offering £500 for the first genuine and clear photograph of the Loch Ness Monster. I could use that money - and so could you, I expect. I'm saving up. Are you? I want a really good cine-camera and projector, and this money would just suit me nicely. It would be fine if I had the cine-camera first, of course - to photograph the Monster. But that can't be helped. I've got quite a good ordinary one, that will have to do. I'm quite certain that the Monster is here, and I've got some ideas about finding it, too.

I need help with the boat and everything, and you are good with boats. Could you come and give me a hand? Please do. I've asked my people, and they are quite willing. We would have great fun. But it's serious, really.

You get here by bus from Inverness. It's down the south side of Loch Ness - not the usual road. Anybody will tell you.

Cheerio,

KEN

P.S. Don't tell anybody about what you're coming for: photographing the Monster, I mean. We don't want competition, as we had with the galleon. Anyway, grown-ups will just laugh as usual. K.R.

P.P.S. Bring a couple of torches, with extra batteries. Also a pair of field-glasses, if you can. I've got the frogman's gear again. A pity Donald couldn't come. K.R.

P.P.P.S. If you come and we get the photo, you can have £150 of the cash. K.R.

Fiona thought that was a pretty good letter, and quite the most exciting she had had for a long time. The £150 would come in useful, too.

2
Ken Thinks it Out

'I'VE seen it! I've seen it!' Ken Rutherford cried, exultantly. He had to shout against the noise of the bus's engine. 'Last night, it was. I'll swear it was it!'

Fiona stepped down from the little bus, bag in hand. 'Hullo, Ken,' she said. 'It's nice to see you.'

'Yes. Look - it's true, Fiona. Nobody believes me, of course, but I'm used to that! I'm certain that it was it. It looked just as they say: four or five humps sticking up above the water, and going at a good speed. A proper wash behind it.'

'Did you get a photo?'

'No. 'Fraid not. It was too far away. And the light wasn't good.'

'Good! I mean, too bad! But... well, I'd like to be there when you get your real picture, Ken.'

'I bet you would! Oh, this is Jakey. He drives the hotel brake. He ghillies, too. This is Fiona MacBride. She's a girl, but she's all right.'

'Hullo, Jakey.'

'Aye then, Miss.'

'Jakey believes in the Monster. Don't you, Jakey?'

'Ooh, aye. Aye.'

'He hasn't seen it yet, but he'd jolly well like to. Wouldn't you, Jakey?'

'Aye. Oooh, aye.'

As they climbed in at the offside of the old shooting-brake, Ken nudged Fiona. 'Jakey only has the one word of conversation,' he whispered, 'but he can say aye in a lot of different ways. He's a wizard driver too.'

The wizardry of Jakey's motoring was made very clear even on the short drive down from the main Stratherrick road-end to the loch-shore. Fiona, who did not get much motoring on her island home of Eorsa, practically held her breath from start to finish. It was left to Ken to do the talking.

This he did, without pause, on the subject of the Monster, its supposed haunts and habits, eye-witnesses' accounts, probable appearance and so on. He scornfully dismissed Nessie as a vulgar and unsuitable name for what was clearly a most noble and masculine creature. Nestor, he thought, was a much more suitable name for something as proud and ancient as the classics themselves. Nestor the Monster of Ness sounded just right, he thought. Ken seemed practically on speaking terms with it.

Ardroy Lodge Hotel sat on a grassy terrace

backed by dark Scots pines, on the very edge of the loch, looking out over a great spread of sparkling blue waters. Fiona's heart sank a little at the sight, thankful as she was to have survived Jakey's wild driving, and beautiful as she admitted the scene to be. There seemed to be a great deal of loch there. She had somehow thought of Loch Ness as rather like one of her own little rocky lochs on Eorsa. This vast expanse was more like the sea that lay between her island and the mainland. It made an awful lot of space in which to look for even an outsize in monsters. She did not say so, of course.

Fiona was warmly welcomed to the hotel by Mrs Rutherford, and later by Ken's father when he came in from fishing the Roybeg River. Nothing was said of Nestor, except for one joking remark by Major Rutherford that he did not know why the Loch area got such a name for monsters, as the biggest thing that he had been able to bring out so far had been barely nine inches long. Ken rather hurriedly turned the conversation into other waters.

The girl was given a little attic room to herself, high up in the roof, where she had a magnificent view over the loch. It occurred to her, as she sat at the window that night, that it was strange that *they* should come to this place, hoping to see the Monster, when the hotel-people who had all this constantly before them had never seen it. Of course it probably was right enough that people who lived with a certain view all the time seldom looked at it. Such notions did not stop her from staring out over the darkening waters long after she should have been asleep - and long after it was possible to see clearly more than a few yards from the shore. By that time, however, Fiona was seeing not only monsters but all sorts of still more curious and alarming things in every ripple and shadow of the loch.

She scuttled into bed, hid her head under the sheets, and dreamed of giant lobsters, out of Donald the fisherman's lobster-pots, chasing her at home on Eorsa.

Without a doubt, Loch Ness was a wonderful loch for looking at. As well as sparkling in the sun, it showed up exciting blue, purple and green colours in different lights, reflecting its different depths; it scowled gloomily under dark clouds, gleamed silver at the least opportunity, and was ruffled by unexpected wind-currents that seemed to come swooping down on it from different hill-tops, making quite big waves in one part while it was smooth as a mirror in another. Ducks flew over it, or paddled in its bays, fish jumped out of it, and occasionally a boat or two passed up or down on its way through the Caledonian Canal. Nonetheless, after two whole days of solid staring from various points where she had been placed by Ken, binoculars in hand, with strict instructions not to move an inch and not to take her eyes off a certain section of water, Fiona began to find that its attractions were fading. She was beginning too to find lights dancing before her eyes.

Though loyal to Ken and his idea, she felt that she had to say something about it that night. They had had a rather difficult time at dinner, with Mrs Rutherford asking all sorts of questions about how they had filled in the day, and whether Fiona was enjoying herself. Ken's hurried but rather vague assurances that they were exploring the district and having lots of fun, did not sound very convincing, and drew an odd look from his mother - who no doubt knew her Ken.

'Look, Ken,' Fiona said afterwards, when they were alone in the garden. 'We can't just go on sitting still and staring at the loch every day. I'm sure that we'll never get anywhere, that way. It's... it's rather a bore, too, isn't it? Really?'

The boy frowned. 'Losing heart already?' he complained. 'It hasn't taken you long, I must say. You can't expect to see the Monster in just the first hour or two of watching.'

'It's been the first twenty hours now!' Fiona pointed out. 'I realize that, Ken; but this just doesn't seem to be the right way to go about it, somehow.'

'What do you suggest then?' he asked, a bit stiffly.

'Well, I don't know, really,' she had to admit.

'But you said in your letter that you had some ideas about finding the Monster?'

'So I have, but that's for when we know roughly in what area Nestor lives. I mean, this loch is twenty-four miles long and a mile wide in most places. That's an enormous lot of water. There's no use in trying out any special ideas until we've narrowed down the area to certain likely spots — that's obvious.'

'Yes, but how on earth are we going to do that? Without seeing the creature, I mean?'

'Well, I've done it already, to some extent,' Ken said. 'I've narrowed it down to these parts where we've been watching these past days. It's still too big an area, of course. We'll have to get a lot closer than that.'

'Closer?'

'Yes. Cut down the area of search, you see.'

'How on earth can we do that? We haven't even had a glimpse of the thing! How can we cut down anything, Ken?'

'Well, I've worked out a theory. I've worked out all the places where Nestor has been seen, and made a sort of plot of them — a chart; also the hour of day, time of year, weather conditions, and so on. It's all jolly interesting. I won't go over it all with you now, but what it boils down to is this. I've come to the conclusion that Nestor lives somewhere up in this section of the loch, south of Craig Point - over there where the cliff is on the other side - and north of Rhumore - that's the wooded headland down on our left there. They're about a mile apart. He's never actually been seen there, mind, but I've noticed that every time he *has* been seen and disturbed, he's headed north or south towards here - never in any other direction, almost. I reckon he's a pretty cute operator, is Nestor - he must be, of course, to have kept himself from being traced all this time; and I believe that he just never surfaces in daylight in his own home area, but does his stuff a good distance from home. This section of the loch is one of the few parts where he has never been seen at all. It's my opinion that that's because this is his home stretch!'

'I say!' Fiona cried. 'That's wonderful - if it's right. But why have we been watching this bit all the time, then? If he's never likely to show up here?'

'Because, don't you see - if we *do* see him in this bit, it proves my theory wrong, and we'll have to start looking somewhere else.'

'My goodness, but that's pretty silly, isn't it? I mean, where on earth does that get us?' the girl objected. 'We're hoping not to see the animal then! What sort of use is that, Ken? I think it's daft!'

'And have you any better suggestion?'

'Well... er... no. I suppose not, but it does seem terribly vague, Ken, doesn't it?'

'*I* don't think so. You see, there's more to it than

just that. I've worked it out that Nestor probably only comes up - or at least only shows himself in daylight - after rough weather. It may be the disturbance that does it. Or perhaps it's the thick floodwaters brought down by the rivers after heavy rain that bring him out. Something does. I'm hoping that one of these sudden storms that we get might bring him up.'

'You said that you thought he didn't *come* up, around here, if this is his home district. You can't have it both ways, Ken.'

'Well, he might just pop up for a sort of quick look-around, you know - before scooting off to whichever end of the loch he chooses for whatever he does when he's on view.' Admittedly Ken sounded rather sheepish as he put this last suggestion forward. He avoided the girl's eye.

Fiona was quite frank. 'I don't think much of that,' she said. 'It strikes me that we're wasting our time, peering at the water all day. Anyway, how can you expect to get a photo of the beast, if it just bobs up for a moment, out in the middle of the loch?'

'It wouldn't necessarily be out in the middle,' Ken pointed out. 'It's quite likely that Nestor actually lives in some underwater rocky cavern, tucked in under one of the banks. It might just as easily be this one as the other. That's not really how I expect to get the photo anyway. I've got a scheme for that. You see - if we can only find out where he does hang out, and it is a disturbance that brings him up - why, then, *we* can create the disturbance!'

'Eh...? We can't whistle up a handy storm, can we?'

'No. But we could set off a small underwater explosion, like those poachers did at Eorsa, that ought to disturb Nestor quite a lot!'

'Oh, I say! That's a notion! D'you think it would work, Ken? I mean, it's not quite the same sort of disturbance, is it?'

'No. It might be enough to arouse the creature none the less. I expect he must just sleep a lot, down there. If he's hundreds of years old, he's bound to be sort of sleepy, by now. Probably storms, or muddy flood-water, wake him up. Our explosion could do the same.'

'Yes. Yes, I see that, but if you don't really think that he ever risks coming up here - to the surface, I mean - what good is that going to do?'

'He doesn't risk coming up in *daylight*, I said - when he could be seen. By night is probably a different matter. I should think he quite often may come up in the darkness, possibly to feed.'

'Could you photograph him by night? In the dark?'

'With a flashbulb - yes. I've got all the gear. I'd need you to work the flash. It's dead-easy - done from a battery.'

'I see. That's a pretty good idea, but we'd have

to get awfully near, wouldn't we?'

'Well, I've got an idea about that, too. You know how all animals and birds - even fishes - are attracted to a light in the darkness. There's no reason why Nestor should be different, is there? If we let a light down, under water, after we'd set off the explosion, then the chances are that he might come along to have a look. We'd keep raising the light to the surface, to coax him up. It's worth a try, don't you think?'

'Yes, indeed. It certainly is. I think that's pretty clever. We'll need a boat...'

'Of course. I've got all that laid on. I've been planning this for ages, you know.'

'Then - what are we waiting for?'

'To know where to let off the confounded explosion!' Ken burst out. 'That's all!'

'Ummmm!' Fiona said.

3
Secret Attempt

SOME time in the middle of that night, Fiona was awakened by something. There was a good lot of noise going on, she found the window rattling, rain blattering against the glass, and the pines outside sobbing and groaning. She was sleepily wondering if it was that that had roused her, when she heard a voice.

'Fiona! Fiona - I say!'

It was Ken, making a sort of whispered shout from the doorway. She sat up.

'What's the matter? Speak up,' she called, yawning. 'I can't hear what you're saying, for all this row.'

'That's the whole point!' he answered, raising his voice. 'It's quite a storm, see. Wind and rain. Just the job - for Nestor!'

'Oh. Oh, yes. Of course. Good. Just as you say.'

'We'll have to get cracking. Early. *Early*, I say.

Yes. Before it's light.'

'Goodness me! Not... not tonight?'

'Yes. Of course. It's a chance. You wouldn't want to lie snoring in bed, would you, with Nestor maybe on view?'

'I don't snore...'

'Never mind that. Don't you want to come?'

'Well...' She swallowed. 'I don't know, exactly,' she said, very doubtfully. 'You mean, out in a *boat*?'

'Yes. Of course. What d'you think?'

'But how?'

'Jakey has a little boat of his own. It's nothing much, but he says I can use it whenever I like.'

'But - in this sort of weather...?'

'It's not the sea, silly! A loch like this will never be really *rough*. I'll come for you about four o'clock. That's in three hours. It's light about six-thirty just now.'

'Oh,' Fiona said, and that sounded just a little like the groaning of the pine trees outside.

Then the door closed, and Ken was gone.

It seemed a lot less than three hours before he was back for her. Muffled up in two jerseys and a rain-coat, Fiona tiptoed downstairs after the boy. Outside it was still windy and wet and cold, and most unpleasant. Ken led the way through the garden and down to the little wooden jetty where the six or seven hotel boats were tied up. These were all bobbing about in lively fashion, with wavelets splashing loudly and even some spray flying on the wind. But even so Fiona had to admit that it was not rough, not as anyone who knew the Hebridean seas thought of roughness. Jakey's boat, smaller and shabbier than the others, was kept apart in a little creek, with oars and row-locks hidden nearby. Ken put his bundle of gear, wrapped in a waterproof, carefully into the stern, and they piled in, each taking an oar - for Fiona was in fact the more practised oarsman of the two. They pushed off into the dark jabbly waters.

'Where do we make for?' the girl asked. It was almost the first thing that she had said. Four o'clock of a wet dark morning was not her best time, cheerful character though she was.

'May as well stick to this side,' Ken answered. 'It's as likely as the other. We'll go down-loch until we're roughly opposite Craig Point, and then just row up and down between there and Rhumore, maybe four hundred yards off shore, keeping our eyes skinned all the time. It's about all we can do. If Nestor's at the other side of the loch - well, we just can't help it. We'll have to try there another time.'

That did not sound a terribly hopeful proposition to Fiona - not enough to justify getting her out of her warm bed - but at least visibility was a lot better than it had seemed from indoors. They could see reasonably well for two hundred yards and more.

Jakey's boat was a light affair, little more than a skiff, and the waves, though small by sea standards, tossed it about as though it had been an egg-shell. It was very easy to pull though, and they slap-slapped along at a good speed, glad of the exercise to keep warm. They quickly got wet, how much from the splash of their rowing and how much from the rain it was hard to say.

They had to slow down when they came level with Craig Point across the loch, since there was no sense in rushing madly up and down their chosen beat. They could not see the far shore, of course, in the gloom, but they knew their landmarks on this side by now. The wind was south-westerly, so that fortunately the waves struck them roughly bows on; it would not have been very pleasant had they come broadside on. They kept a course about three hundred yards offshore, and rowed slowly but steadily, taking turns at peering out on different sides.

They could see better than Fiona had expected, but even so it was not a simple matter to scan the surface thoroughly. The water looked inky black, and it had not a phosphorescent gleam like the sea. The waves made a certain amount of foam and white veining, but not enough really to break up the dark background so that anything solid might be outlined clearly against it. They could see for quite a distance, but there was no certainty or shape about what they saw.

'Do you think we'd really see the Monster in this - make it out, I mean - even if it did come up?' Fiona wondered. 'Everything is so dim and vague.'

'We'd see Nestor himself, I think, if he broke surface,' Ken answered. 'Whether we'd see his wash, which is what I'm really looking for, I don't know.'

'Wash? But isn't your explosion meant to do more than that?'

'We're not letting off the explosion tonight, mutt!' the boy exclaimed. 'This storm should have done all the disturbing that's necessary. It's been blowing for hours now. I'm hoping that Nestor was roused hours ago, and has been away up or down the loch, feeding or whatever it is he does. We're really looking for him coming back. Coming home, see?'

'Oh. Oh, well. But, still...'

'What I really would like is to catch a glimpse of him coming back, even just his wash, so as to note where he goes down and then come back another night with the explosive and the light, to try to bring him up again.'

They rowed down as far as the jutting headland of Rhumore, and then turned to pull back. The wind was with them now, but that meant of course that the rain was in their faces as they rowed, making observation still more difficult.

Half-way back to their starting-point, Fiona suddenly stopped pulling. 'Look, Ken - there!' she cried, and pointed. 'You see? Just over there - between us and that line of foam. You *must* see it!'

'I do, yes. I see it. I see something, anyway. Quick - you take my oar, Fiona. Pull towards it. Don't splash, if you can help it. I'll get the camera out, and the bulb, just in case.'

Closer inspection however showed them only a drifting waterlogged tree-trunk, and their excitement went flat.

So up and down they rowed, staring, peering, hoping - and getting colder and wetter. Ken reckoned that from their beat they were able to see practically half-way across the loch. Admittedly the Monster had been seen more often on that other side, but then the main road ran along that shore, and so a lot more people would have been in a position to see it from there. Perhaps they were doing the wrong thing in sticking to this south side? But it was a toss-up either way.

Slowly the light began to increase, so gradually that they did not notice it until suddenly they realized that they could see the far shore. In the grey half-light it seemed almost more difficult than ever to distinguish anything in detail. Their watches said that it was six-thirty.

'We'll give it just half an hour more,' Ken said,

frowning. 'We don't want the whole hotel awake when we get back, or everyone will have to hear what we're doing.'

By seven o'clock, when they tied up Jakey's boat in its creek, they were no further forward. Somewhat gloomily they made for the back door of the hotel. The wind was dropping, but it was still raining.

Fortunately they saw only Jakey as they crept indoors - he was Boots amongst his other duties, and was busy collecting shoes from outside bedroom doors. Whispering, they informed him of Nestor's lack of co-operation.

'Aye,' he said, nodding seriously. 'Uh-huh. Ooh, aye.'

They left it at that.

Two of the hotel guests were very late for breakfast, a couple of hours later. Mrs Rutherford, at Fiona's fifth yawn, asked kindly if she had had a disturbed night with the wind. Fiona thought that she could quite honestly admit to something of the sort.

At dinner that night, after a dull day of rain, it was Major Rutherford's turn to arrive late, damp but cheerful. He had had an excellent day's fishing on the swollen Roybeg River, and proceeded to inform the party in some detail of each fish and how he had hooked, played, outwitted and landed it.

Since he had caught no fewer than fifteen, this took some time, and they were all having coffee in the lounge, with the young people rather eager to be elsewhere, when he worked up to a finish.

'So I squeezed him into the basket, and I had to rearrange the others like sardines in a tin to get him in at all,' he declared. 'I could hardly lift the basket on to my shoulder, for the weight. You needn't look so superior and unbelieving, young Ken! It's a fact, and they're all through there in the kitchen to prove it. Not like this latest tall tale about the Monster. Of all the...'

'Eh? What's that, Daddy?' Hastily Ken swallowed, and tried to disguise the eagerness in his voice. 'Has... did you say there's something new about Nest... about Nessie?'

'Haven't you heard? Somebody claims to have seen the thing last night. Or at least, early this morning - though it all sounds typically fishy and unlikely to me.'

'Where?' Fiona gasped.

'Oh, well,' Major Rutherford coughed. 'It was actually up in the little pub at the road-end. I'd just slipped in for a moment, you see - being pretty wet. Keep out the cold, and all that...'

'I don't mean that,' Fiona began, when Ken silenced her with a glance.

'Yes, dear. Quite,' Mrs Rutherford said to her husband, smiling.

'Er... well, they told me in there. Some character called Murdo the Croft is saying that he saw the creature in the early hours of this morning. You'd wonder what he was doing out at that time, wouldn't you! He says apparently that he was looking for a lost collie pup. A likely story! I expect he either dreamed the whole thing, or was drunk enough to see pink elephants as well. The people in the pub admit that he's no teetotaller. An old man...'

'Did he say anything about it?' Ken asked, as casually as he could. 'Give any details?'

'I don't know. I dare say he may have claimed it to have had a red beard and tartan stripes! I didn't ask, laddie.'

'No. Sure, Dad. Mum, can we go now? Fiona and I have... er, something to do.'

'Of course. Run along. But don't be too late back.'

4
Getting Murdo to Talk

'YOU know this man, this Murdo the Croft, Jakey?'

'Aye, then.'

'And is it right that he drinks? A lot, I mean? Gets drunk?'

Jakey sighed. 'Aye,' he said.

'But I expect that he sometimes tells the truth, just the same?'

'Oh, aye. Sure. Aye.'

'Do you think it's true that he saw the Monster last night?'

'Oh, aye.'

'No, but *really*, Jakey?'

'Och, well,' the other said, driven into a corner, as it were.

'I wish...' Ken began, and then catching Fiona's eye, stopped himself. 'You'll know where he lives, at least?'

'Oooh, aye.'

'Could you manage to take us there? It will be on this side of the loch, at any rate? Is it far?'

'No,' said Jakey - and that from him made a nice change.

'Good, then. Let's go.'

Jakey led them down the loch-shore for about two miles till they came to a little tumble-down cottage amongst some tiny brackeny fields and a good deal of old iron. A sheep collie and two pups came barking to meet them, and the noise brought to the door of the croft-house an elderly bent man in shirt-sleeves, whose patched and faded plus-fours hung right down to his boots. He had extraordinarily blue eyes, Fiona noticed, and they looked keen enough.

'You will be Mr Murdo the Croft?' Ken said politely. 'I expect you know Jakey? I'm Ken Rutherford, and this is Fiona.'

'Is that so? Just that,' the other nodded. 'A very fine night it would be, if it was not for the rain, just.'

'Well, I suppose so,' Ken answered doubtfully.

'It'll maybe fair up sometime, and then it will be grand - just grand,' the old man suggested hopefully; and all in the same breath he added, 'You will be from the hotel, then? If it is the Monster, see you, I'm not saying a word. Och, not a word, at all.'

'But,' Ken gulped. 'Oh, I say! That's - that's not

fair! I mean, we've come specially.'

'I well believe it - I do so! But, och, that's the way of it, just. Not a word.'

'But...' Ken found Fiona's hand on his arm, and paused.

'I expect you're just tired of people asking silly questions, Mr Murdo?' she said sympathetically.

'Indeed I am that, lassie,' the old crofter agreed. 'My Chove, yes! Here's me just wishing I had never seen the beastie, at all!'

'Then you *did* see it?'

'Mercy to goodness - of course I did! As plain as my own nose, whatever.'

'Yes - we were sure you had. Other people don't seem to believe it, somehow - but we did. People are terribly unbelieving, aren't they?'

'Indeed and that's a fact, Missie. You're right there. The unbelievability of people is wicked, just wicked! Here's me no further away from the creature than your own self, and them trying to tell me that I was after seeing a string of ducks, or a bit of wood, or a pair of otters, even. Och, otters with a horse's face on them!'

'A *horse's* face? Did it look like a horse, then?' Ken cried.

'Aye it did. Och... well, maybe. Something like that. But I'm not saying any more, boy, I am not,' Murdo declared, remembering.

Fiona stepped in again swiftly. 'I don't blame

you, either,' she said warmly. 'I think you're quite right. After all, you'll just get folk saying that you were seeing things, or had had a glass too much, or something rude like that.'

'My Chove, I was stone-cold sober, just!' the other interrupted hotly. 'Not a drink had I in me. There was myself coming along the shore, just, by Rhubeg, and there of a sudden was a great wave coming up the loch - och, like behind a motor-boat it was. At this small bit of a headland there - at Rhubeg - the wave turns, see you. Turns to the shore. And just as it comes near in, up comes a horse's head on a long neck, like. Och, long, long the neck was. Then Sheila - that's the collie, there - begins a great noise of barking, and, och, the creature near exploded, just! The Monster, I mean. A right fright it got. Round about it birled, to get away back. Dearie me, the splashing! And the size of it! I tell you, it was fair mountainous!'

'You actually saw more than just the head and neck, then?'

'Indeed I did, lassie. As it turned round, see you. Mind, it was dark, and there was a right splatter of water, but och, I'd say the body was twicc as thick as Jeannie the cow, there. Och, easy that. And long. I didn't see any end to it.'

'By Jove!' Ken gasped. 'This is wonderful! And do you think it was coming in to land, Mr... er, Murdo?'

'Aye, it looked that way. But... och,' the old man frowned and shook his head. As before, when it was the boy who questioned him, he seemed to remember his decision not to talk. 'I'm no' saying another word,' he declared strongly. 'I said so to those men from the newspapers, and that goes for you too, my goodness!'

Fiona smiled in her most winning way. 'We quite understand how you feel,' she said. 'We won't ask any more questions, will we, Ken? After all, you would only see the beast for a moment, anyway.'

'I did not see it only for a moment, just!' the little man protested. 'I saw it, och, for quite a whilie.'

'Even when it swam away out into the middle of the loch?'

'It didn't swim out into the middle. It swam round the side, just. Round this bit of a headland of Rhubeg. Down into the little small bay below. And then it went round and round in a sort of a circle. Two or three times. And then it was gone.'

'Gone? You mean, it dived?'

'Och, I couldn't say, just. I didn't see what it did. But it wasn't there any more, at all.'

'It swam round in a circle two or three times, and then dived?' Ken repeated. 'In this little bay? I say - that's pretty important, I think! If...'

'I don't think that we ought to trouble Murdo any more,' Fiona broke in hurriedly. 'I'm sure that he doesn't want to say anything about it. We'll just leave him in peace. I expect Jakey knows this Rhubeg headland?'

'Oh, aye.'

'That's fine, then. You've been awfully patient with us, Mr Murdo. I do hope that nobody else comes and bothers you - then you can forget the whole thing.'

'Just that, lassie. I'm no' saying a word, mind - no' a single cheep!'

'No. Quite. Well - good night.'

'Er, good night,' Ken added. 'The bay south of this Rhubeg, it was?'

'Aha, laddie - you'll no' catch me that way! I'm no' telling a single thing, at all.'

'Oh, well. Thanks. Goodbye.'

'Aye, then,' Jakey observed.

They had no difficulty in finding Rhubeg, a green tree-clad headland, and the deep little bay just to the south; there was nothing of the sort to the north. Ken was tremendously excited.

'It's a wonderful stroke of luck,' he cried, 'that old Murdo saw Nestor turn into this bay, and circle round before diving. There's a jolly good chance that this is his home - this bay. It's deep-looking, too, judging by the colour of the water. Look!' Stooping he picked up a large stone and threw it out as far as he could. It fell with a heavy leaden plonk that seemed to speak of great depth. 'You see! This may well be just what we've been looking for.'

'I think it might be, too,' Fiona nodded, not bothering to point out that she had thought so from the first mention of the bay by Murdo the Croft.

'It's just about half a mile further down the loch from where we ended our beat, last night,' Ken went on. 'If we'd only come a little further down! It would be about the same time of night, too. Nestor would be on his way home, just as I calculated. I expect old Munro was out poaching - one reason why he won't want to say too much about it!'

'Naturally,' the girl agreed. 'I was allowing for that when I was talking to him - hoping that you wouldn't ask him *why* he was there.'

'I wouldn't have done that. I'm not a complete ass, you know. A queer old bird, isn't he?'

'I think he's nice.'

'Well, he certainly seemed nicer to you than to me! I think you handled him pretty well, on the whole, for a girl!'

Fiona looked at Jakey, and solemnly winked one eye.

That upstanding youth blinked, flushed pink, and took a deep breath. 'Aye!' he got out, with much feeling.

'Tomorrow night, then,' Ken declared. 'We'll have a go. Mum and Dad are going out to dinner at Fort Augustus. It's a chance...'

5
Fishing for Trouble

THE following evening once again Jakey's boat pulled out into Loch Ness with its crew of two. Major and Mrs Rutherford being away out for dinner meant that awkward explanations were not necessary; they were not expected to be back till after midnight, so that the young people had over three hours - which surely ought to be enough for their experiment? They had quite a lot of bulky gear to stow in the stern, however, and getting it down to the boat without attracting the attention of other hotel guests was quite a problem.

It was a dull September night, but fair, with the loch calm, and they put off their departure till eight o'clock when it was as dark as it would get. They did not want anybody to see their entry to the little bay below Rhubeg. They saw the gleam of lamp-light from Murdo the Croft's cottage as they rowed southwards, but otherwise all was gloom.

The bay was easily found. It was no more than two hundred yards across and thrust almost the same distance inland. There was no beach here, only steep rocky banks dropping sheer into the water. Ken pulled up as nearly in the centre of the bay as he could judge.

'Now, to get busy!' he cried.

First of all they let down a heavy leaden weight on the longest piece of fishing-line that they had. There was fully three hundred feet of this, and when still the weight did not touch bottom when it was fully run out, Ken was satisfied.

'Grand! It's deep enough, anyway,' he said. 'If it had turned out to be a fairly shallow bay after all, we could have packed up - for it's fairly certain that Nestor won't live in any shallow bit. Now we can try out the light.'

Ken had made a rather cunning underwater lamp out of two six-volt dry cells and four of the strongest bicycle-torch bulbs and reflectors, all bottled up inside a small goldfish bowl that he had bought in Inverness, the mouth tightly covered with plastic and coated thickly with grease to keep the water out. It shone brightly in all directions, like a little light-house, and glowed in a most ghostly fashion when they lowered it on a long cord into the dark water. It got vaguer and dimmer as it sank, and by a hundred feet they could not see it any more.

'Do you think that will do?' Fiona wondered. 'I

mean, if *we* can't see it at more than a hundred feet - that's only thirty yards or so - then maybe the Monster won't be able to see it from very far either? I'd have thought it would have shone further than that.'

'It's the peat in the water,' Ken explained. 'It's very brown and dims the lamp. I think that Nestor's underwater vision will be a mighty lot better than ours. Down there, that light will probably show much further than from up here. I hope so, anyway - for the loch is at least six hundred feet deep in the middle, and though I don't suppose it's so much inshore here, it still leaves an awful lot of water below our lamp. We can always add a bit more to the cord.'

They experimented with raising and lowering the lamp for a bit, and as far as that went it seemed to work perfectly.

'Now for the explosive,' Ken said. 'I've had to concoct a waterproof jar for that, too. Fortunately, ordinary two pound jam jars are good enough for this.'

'How did you get it?' the girl asked. 'The explosive, I mean? Was it awfully difficult?'

'Easy as winking,' she was told. 'I just bought a box of 25 twelve-bore shot-gun cartridges, and emptied out the gunpowder from each cartridge into a jam jar. It about quarter-fills it - which leaves plenty of air. I've stuck in a length of safety-fuse -

and there we are. It was expensive, though - for I've made three of these bombs, and each box of cartridges costs 14/-. What with one thing and another, I've spent over £4 on this business, so we'd better win that £500 or I shall be bankrupt!'

'I think you've been very clever,' Fiona assured him. 'I'd never have thought of all this. But... you don't think all this gunpowder, this explosion, could do any harm? I mean, it couldn't possibly *hurt* the Monster, could it?'

'Of course not, silly! That amount of loose powder will only make a loud bang, under water. It won't even sound very loud from up here. It's not like dynamite or gelignite. In fact, I'm just hoping that it's powerful enough to make a real disturbance... though not powerful enough to damage fish. That's a thing I've had to think about.'

Ken got everything ready, attaching a heavy weight to the jar to sink it, and then lit the safety-fuse. Fumbling a little with excitement, he replaced the water-tight lid, smeared it with grease, and lowered it over the side.

'I made it a three-minute fuse, to give us plenty of time,' he said, paying out the line hurriedly. 'All the same...'

To Fiona at least it seemed a long three minutes. Even after Ken had come to the end of his line, they had to sit and wait. 'I think something's gone wrong,' she said at last, panting a little through holding her breath. 'Surely it should have gone off by now?'

'You know what it's like at the Two Minutes' Silence on Remembrance Day - how long that seems,' Ken pointed out. But he sounded a little bit doubtful himself. 'It's maybe just as well that I kept it on a string. I half thought of just throwing the thing overboard loose, to let it sink on its own and explode at whatever depth it reached, but I decided that I couldn't risk losing it altogether if something went wrong...'

The boy's voice tailed away as suddenly the boat seemed to rise beneath them. There was nothing violent or dramatic about it; the skiff just quietly lifted up and up. The water too was rising around them in a circle that had become pale, streaked with white, almost as though it were boiling and seething. There was a strange hissing noise, and then through it a deep grumbling sound. That was all - no bang, no waterspout. Then the level of the loch around them sank back, and the boat with it - probably it had not risen more than a couple of feet - the white faded, and two or three waves rolled away from them to break after a moment or two on the rocky beach with a sad sigh. The boat rocked and dipped gently.

'Goodness!' Fiona cried. 'Was that it? Is that all? That wasn't enough noise to - to waken a baby!'

'Well...' Ken began, clearing his throat. 'Hang it

all - it wasn't a depth-charge, you know! Though, I must say, I thought it would have been more... more sort of impressive, myself! Of course, it's not the noise it makes up here that is important, but the disturbance down below. I know that shock-waves travel a tremendous distance and with great force under water - that's how asdics and echo-sounders and so on work. Noise probably isn't the main thing, at all, but shock-waves. I dare say that explosion would reach Nestor all right - if he's anywhere about here at all.'

'M'mmm,' Fiona said, uncertainly. 'Well... maybe. At least, it oughtn't to have killed any fish!'

'We'll just have to hope for the best, anyway. I've got two more of these charges. I suppose we could let them both down at once, and make double the explosion, but that would be the end of my gunpowder- and it's dashed expensive buying more cartridges.'

'Well, let's not worry about that just now,' the girl suggested. 'Should we not put the lamp down now?'

'Oh, yes. Sure. That's the next stage.'

They switched on the lights and lowered the lamp down as far as it would go. Ken handed the line over to the girl, telling her to keep raising and lowering it slowly, almost up to the surface and down again. He began to fit up the flash-bulb apparatus for the camera, and explained, not for the first time, just how it was to be worked. He intended to do the actual photographing himself if possible, but one of them might have to row to get near enough if the beast came up, and they must both be prepared to do one job or the other. Anything that they did would almost certainly have to be done pretty fast. There would be no time for discussion.

They waited for a bit, Fiona busy with her line.

'How long do you think it will take,' she asked, 'if he's going to come at all?'

'I haven't a clue,' the boy admitted. 'It could all depend on a dozen things.' He peered towards the shore. 'You don't think we're drifting much, do you?'

'I shouldn't think so. There's no wind.' She turned to look the other way, across the loch. 'Oh-o-o-oh!' she cried - and that was next thing to a scream. 'Look! Look!' The string of the lamp slipped out and away from fingers suddenly gone nerveless.

6
Enter the Monster

NOT ten yards from the boat, on the far side, quite the most extraordinary creature that either of them had ever seen or imagined was staring at them. Silent, still, absolutely motionless, as though it had been there for hours, what looked for all the world like an enormous snail reared itself out of the water. It appeared to be only a neck and head that they were seeing, but these rose fully five feet into the air. Almost like an immensely thick periscope the neck rose, three times as thick as any elephant's trunk; and on top was a comparatively small flat-tish head sprouting two little horn-like knobs where ears might have been, perked forward like those of a snail. It was too dark to see much in the way of detail, but the colour appeared to be dark grey and the skin rough without being hairy. But it was the great oval flat-looking eyes, glowing dully at them, that held the young people's startled gaze. Unblinking, utterly without movement or expression, these stared - and the effect was alarming.

As though paralysed Ken and Fiona sat, all their plans of action for the moment shocked out of them. They hardly dared to breathe. It is one thing to decide to raise the devil and another altogether when he is looking at you only a few yards away.

Ken recovered first, in a sort of way.

'Oh! Ah... gosh! Quick!' he gulped. 'By Jove! It's... it's... oh, my goodness!' He pointed a trembling finger, which was not what he had intended to do at all.

Fiona nodded, dumbly.

Then they had some movement, at last. Whether it was the boy's move that set off the Monster, or the other way round, would be hard to say. At any rate the creature dipped its head towards them with a snake-like coiling of its long neck, almost at the same moment that Ken dived for the camera. Fiona yelled.

After that, things happened too fast to be set down in any proper order. The water on the other, landward, side of the skiff suddenly began to churn up wildly, and the boat started to tip up on its end. It did not rise gently, smoothly, as when raised by the underwater explosion, but crazily, with a bump and a rush, Fiona was flung headlong into the stern, and a moment later Ken tumbled down on top of her.

The little craft was not built to stand this sort of thing, and a couple of seconds later, its stern dipping still further, both boy and girl were in the water.

The shock of the cold brought Fiona very much to her senses. She could swim like a fish, and was not in the least worried about drowning, but the thought of being in the water with that Monster was not pleasant. She splashed about furiously. It did not take her long to realize however that her feeble efforts were as nothing in the storm of splashing that was going on around her. Clearly it was not Ken's doing, either. All this churning, foaming whirlpool was caused by something infinitely bigger than either of them.

That notion really terrified the girl. When a moment later she felt herself being pushed over and over by something extremely large and solid, she lost her head again altogether for a little, and struck out blindly with a desperate urge to escape, to leave this awful spot, to reach dry land.

Madly she swam - but not for long. For one thing, she was not sure that she was going in the right direction, for she could see little for spray and splatter. For another, she remembered that the banks of the bay were steep - almost small cliffs. Thirdly, she remembered Ken, who might be in difficulties and need help. Lastly, she caught a glimpse of the boat, still floating, bobbing about on the waves only a few yards away. With a really tremendous effort she tried to swallow her panic, and use her head. Then she realized that the splashing had stopped, and the turmoil of the water was sinking. Had the Monster gone? Had it dived? Treading water, and peering around, she could see no sign of it, unless it was at the other side of the boat again. She saw Ken, quite close at hand, swimming.

'The boat...!' she gasped.

'Yes, yes,' he called back. 'You... all right?'

They swam back to the boat, which lay fairly low in the water.

'I'll hold... the bows down... while you climb in... at the stern,' Ken panted. 'The Monster's gone, I think.'

Fiona hoisted herself aboard with a bit of difficulty, owing to the weight of her sodden clothing. Then she weighted the stern down while the boy climbed in at the other end. They found the skiff to be almost half-full of water.

'Have to bale this out. If the baler isn't gone. I wonder...?' Ken stopped. 'Oh, gosh!'

The Monster was back exactly where it had been before, in the same attitude, watching them as though nothing had happened.

Horrified the boy and the girl stared back.

How long they gazed thus, the young people had no idea. They just sat, too scared to stir, to speak, to take any slightest action, in case they set the creature off again. The Monster seemed as though carved in stone itself. Fiona could distinctly hear wild duck quacking from somewhere down the loch.

When some unknown time had passed, the girl licked her lips. 'Ken,' she whispered, 'the camera!'

'Don't know... where it is,' he answered, below his breath. 'Maybe... under the water, in the boat. Maybe... in the loch.'

'Do you think...? What are we to do?'

'I don't know. Perhaps if we sit quiet, it will go away.'

'But... the photo?'

'I know. But what *can* we do? I think it was me moving that set it off before.'

'Couldn't you move terribly slowly? So that it wouldn't notice, maybe? Down on to the floor-boards. Try to find the camera? Will it be ruined?'

'Don't know. It's worth trying, maybe. It's a risk, to move...'

'Yes. We can't just sit here all night.'

Infinitely slowly, cautiously, the boy began to sink down, lowering himself gradually into the bottom of the little boat, with the water slopping about him. The Monster showed no reaction. An inch at a time he groped along the floorboards. 'Here's the baler, at least,' he reported. 'It's caught, here. Yes - got it. The camera.' As slowly, he rose to his seat on the thwart.

'He hasn't stirred. Not a move,' Fiona told him, softly.

'Good. But this is no use. The flash-bulb's broken.'

'Haven't you got another one?'

'Yes. But it's not just the bulb. The mechanism seems to be bust. I think I must have fallen on top of it. Anyway, probably the spool in the camera's soaked and useless.'

'Oh, what a shame, Ken! What rotten luck! It's hopeless, then?'

''Fraid so. Nothing we can do... but wait.'

That they did, sitting stock-still on their thwarts. It was a very strange business to be sitting there doing absolutely nothing but outstaring the Loch Ness Monster, but at least they were getting an excellent view of the creature. It seemed to be sitting just a little higher in the water now, and what appeared to be the tops of three humps showed behind it, the middle one being highest out of the water. It was hard to tell just how far apart these humps might be, since the animal was facing them head-on, but they certainly gave the impression of an enormous body under the water.

After a bit, for no apparent reason, the Monster suddenly seemed to grow tired of just staring. It coiled down its neck again. The boy and girl crouched, tightly grasping the sides of the boat in case once more the little craft was overthrown. This time however the creature swirled right round in a very narrow semi-circle, at great speed and setting up an impressive bow-wave, to head out towards the middle of the loch. The animal's three humps were now revealed as large, the centre one standing fully four feet out of the water and being at least as long as their boat itself. What was more, the gap between each hump was almost as long. Moreover, from the violent commotion in the water quite a long way behind, it was clear either that the body reached a lot further back under water, or else that there was a very powerful and active tail propelling the thing along.

'By Jove - see that!' Ken cried, all need for whispering now over. 'D'you see the size of it? Those humps must be eight or nine feet long - the middle one is, anyway. And they're that distance apart, too! And that tail, or whatever it is, at the back! The thing must be almost fifty feet long!'

'What a speed it's going at!' Fiona gasped. 'Goodness - it's going faster than any motor-boat! It must...' The rest of whatever she was going to say was lost when the little boat suddenly began to heave and toss as the wash of the Monster's passage reached it. For a moment or two it looked as though they might be swamped - as they would have been had they been broadside on to the waves.

By the time that the young people were able to

return their attention to the Monster, it was disappearing into the gloom of the night, head and neck apparently lowered and only the three humps showing, leaving a tremendous turmoil of white water behind it and a great spreading wedge of wake. The white was visible for quite a time after they could no longer see the humps.

'Well! Thank goodness it didn't decide to ram us!' Ken declared. 'It's as fast as a naval destroyer!'

'What a - a crittur! Fancy anyone calling that Nessie! Golly - I got a fright when the boat started to stand on end, that time! And when we were flung into the water, among all that splashing, I thought our last moments had come!'

'It was when the thing bumped into me, under water, that I was most scared,' the girl said, with something between a giggle and a gulp. 'It felt like the side of a house birling me over and over. Or, at least, a submarine, maybe.'

'It did that to me too,' Ken agreed. 'Gosh - that means that we've actually touched it! I don't suppose anybody has ever touched the Loch Ness Monster before!'

'And I for one don't want to do so again,' Fiona answered definitely. 'How did it happen, Ken? I mean, how did the boat get lifted up that way? The thing - Nestor - was away over there when it happened. There couldn't have been *two* of them?'

'I don't think so. There may be more than one -

but not just now. It must have been lying this way. It was facing us, so we assumed that the body lay the other way - away from us. The head must have been twisted round to look back at us. I saw a churning of water on this landward side of the boat. That must have been its tail. It's so huge, you see. Some bit of its body must have been right underneath us. Maybe it didn't mean to attack us, at all. You saw how its humps came up when it went away just now? Maybe my movement to get the camera alarmed it, and it was one of these humps rising up under us that capsized the boat.'

'Yes. Maybe. But... oh, dear - what a shame that you didn't get a photo, Ken.'

He shrugged. 'Can't be helped. One of those things. What do we do now? Get back to the hotel, I suppose?'

It was then that they discovered that they had only one oar. The other presumably had gone overboard at the upset. They peered about, but could see no sign of it. The boat was not one that could be sculled by a single oar over the stern; but it was light, and they might be able to paddle it over to the little headland, using loose floorboards: that is, when it was baled out and less heavy.

They started to bale, Ken with the old rusty tin that served as baler, and Fiona with her cupped hands. It was slow, tiring work, but they were quite glad of the activity, for now they discovered that they were shivering with cold and wet.

It took them some time to empty the boat. When they had almost finished, Fiona happened to glance aside. 'Heavens!' she exclaimed. 'It's back!'

The Monster was sitting watching them again, apparently exactly where it had been before. It must have come back almost as fast as it went, but a great deal more quietly, stealthily. No wash had warned them. There it sat, or floated, or whatever it did, evidently much interested. They even got the notion that it cocked its small head to one side as it watched them.

'Mercy - that was pretty sharp!' Ken whispered. 'Sneaking back like that, without a sound! What a funny beast!'

'It seems to find us an attraction, anyway!' Fiona murmured. 'What now?'

'Well, we can't just play I-Spy with it all night.'

'No. Look - is that not our oar, just over there between us and—and it?'

'Where? Oh, yes. I think it is. I wonder... if we moved over to try to get it? What would happen?'

'Goodness knows. Maybe the same thing as before. Maybe nothing.'

'Ummm.'

'It's Jakey's oar. We'll have to get it back to him.'

'That's true. Well, let's try it. Very softly.'

Cautiously they picked up a couple of the floor-boards, slowly lowered them over the side and began very gently to paddle forward with them, clumsy as they were.

The Monster did not make any move during the first three or four yards of their progress. Then as gently and quietly as themselves, it slowly sank its head down and down, till, without so much as a ripple, the dark waters closed over it. Without the least sign or sound the great body sank away. It might never have been there.

It seemed impossible that anything so huge, and that had made so much fuss and splash in its movements before, should have been able to disappear so silently as that. The young people waited, hearts in their mouths lest the creature should come up underneath them, but nothing happened.

'It looks as though it's gone this time,' Ken said at length. 'Would you have believed that anything could have just vanished like that?'

They picked up the missing oar. Since there did not seem to be anything else to do, they began to row back towards the hotel, tongues busy.

As they walked up, wet and stiff, from the jetty, Ken paused in their excited chatter to speak differently. 'You know,' he said, 'I don't think we ought to say anything about all this to the parents. Not yet, anyway. They probably wouldn't believe us, in the first place - they'd think we'd been imagining things. You know the way they do. And in the second place, it's likely they wouldn't let us have another go. Get into a flap about safety, and all that.' He peered at his wrist-watch, and then put it to his ear. 'Good. It doesn't seem to have stopped, despite being in the water. It's not quite midnight. They won't be back yet.'

'You do intend to have another go, then, Ken?'

'Of course I do. What do you take me for? Would *you* give up now?'

'No,' Fiona had to admit. 'I don't suppose I would.'

'Well, then. Now - not a word as we go in.'

Fiona had just a word or two, nevertheless, as they parted outside their rooms. 'You know, Ken,' she whispered, 'I have a sort of idea that Nestor quite likes us. Don't you?'

7
Getting Friendly

IT was not so easy, of course, just to have another go, or even to keep from telling Major and Mrs Rutherford about their exciting experience. It seemed awful for Ken and Fiona to go through that next day without saying a word to anybody about having seen and indeed touched the famous Loch Ness Monster - except to Jakey, who was sworn to secrecy, but who for all that did not make a very rewarding sort of listener, with his comments limited to a lot of ooohs and ayes on various keys. Another attempt at raising Nestor for photographic purposes meant, of course, that they had to be re-equipped.

Fiona had let the underwater lamp slip and sink when first she had seen the Monster, so that a new one had to be made - and goldfish bowls did not grow on Highland hillsides. The film in Ken's camera proved to be useless through being soaked, and though the boy was able to repair the flash-bulb apparatus himself, one of his two spare bulbs rattled ominously and probably wouldn't work. All this meant a trip to Inverness for supplies - and what was worse, it meant money. Ken had very little cash left, and Fiona had little money either. By clubbing together, and being sparing about what they bought, they reckoned that they could just about rake up enough for absolute essentials. If only they could have got a small advance from Major Rutherford on that £500 - but that would mean telling the whole story...

Fortunately they were able to save the double bus fare by getting a lift, on Jakey's advice, in a lorry which went to Inverness and back every day with salmon collected from the various fishing hotels.

So, two days later, all was ready for their second attempt. This time Ken's father and mother were not going to be out in the evening, so that there was nothing for it but to ask their permission to go out in the boat in the dark. At a loss to think of any other excuse to offer, they fell back on the simplest explanation of all - the plain truth. They said that they had heard that the famous Loch Ness Monster was in the habit of coming up in the dark, that night was the best time to see it, and they thought that they would have more chance of seeing it from a boat than on land. Major Rutherford laughed, and said that while he'd believe anything of Ken, he had thought that Fiona would have more sense; but on being pressed, he did not object to them wasting their time, so long as there was no nonsense, and no illegal fishing - for the Fishery Board did not allow angling on the loch after 8pm. Mrs Rutherford smilingly agreed, but said that they were to be very careful and not to be home late; she knew that Fiona was expert with boats, and relied on her to keep Ken out of mischief. It was as easy as that.

In fact, Fiona would have told Ken's people all about what they were up to from the beginning, and risked being laughed at, but the boy insisted that the whole thing must be kept secret or other people would be coming along and following them up, trying to get that photograph and the £500. His father, scoffing as he was about the Monster's existence, would be sure to tell others. It was secrecy or nothing, he said.

As soon as they could get away after dinner, then, they hurried down to the little jetty and this time Major and Mrs Rutherford actually came along to see them embark. It was as well that they had taken down most of their gear beforehand, and stored it under an old waterproof in the stern, or there might have been some difficult questions to answer. As it was, they had to listen straight-faced to a lot of leg-pulling about not letting the Monster bite them or carry them off to some underwater cavern, and so on, before they could pull away. Ken was very apologetic about his father.

'He has a heart of gold,' he explained, 'but he's sort of unimaginative about some things. Down to earth, you know.' He grinned. 'Maybe being a farmer has something to do with it!'

'Perhaps it's having been father to Ken Rutherford for so long that's done it?' Fiona suggested wisely. 'Sort of self-protection.'

The boy looked at her doubtfully, and went on rowing.

It was a fine night and not so dark as last time when they reached their bay below Rhubeg. It was a little earlier too. Ken felt that it was really a bit too early to start operations, but he wanted to test the new underwater lamp that he had had to make; they could do that easily while they were waiting.

The lamp was not as good a job as the first one. Two of its four bulbs did not work very well, and the young people spent quite a time fiddling about with it in the boat before letting it down over the side. Then, as it kept going off and on under water, they had to raise and lower it for adjustments a number of times before they could be satisfied that it was working properly. It was while they were doing this that Ken suddenly spoke differently.

'Listen!' he said. 'Do you hear voices?'

'I thought I did, before,' the girl admitted. 'I wasn't sure, so I didn't say anything. About five minutes ago.'

'They sounded to me... I say, there they are again! Men's voices. On the shore, somewhere. Quite close.'

'Yes, but sounds can carry a long way over water, you know - especially on a still night. It will just be somebody from a car up at the road.'

'No. It's nearer than that, I'm sure. If anybody is near the shore, there, they probably can see us, especially with this light. We had better keep it well down, under water, just now.'

'Does it matter so much, Ken?'

'Yes, it does. We don't want people getting the hang of what we're doing here, or we'll have lots of others trying the same game, and that would probably scare off Nestor. We don't want somebody else beating us to that £500. That's why I've been so anxious not even to let Dad and Mum know.' Ken was whispering now. 'Even if they don't realize what we're doing, really, people might talk. They probably would think that we were poaching, after the eight o'clock limit. We might get landed into all sorts of bother. I...'

A slight but distinct wave rocked the boat, which had up till now been lying entirely still on the calm water. Ken whipped round.

'Gosh! It's... it's him!' he gasped. 'Nestor - back again! Already.'

Sure enough, sitting in roughly the same position and attitude as before, only a little higher in the water this time, so that all three humps showed clearly, was the Monster. It was gazing at them, small head cocked to one side again, with every appearance of interest.

'Goodness!' Fiona exclaimed, voices ashore forgotten. 'The light! The lamp must have brought him up... without any explosion.'

'Yes. Expect so. This is super! Look at his ears, or horns, or whatever they are!'

'I think he's sweet! I'm sure he likes us. He's jolly interested, anyway. Maybe he's even been looking for us, after that last time. I like the way he cocks his head...'

They were both calling it 'him' now, instead of 'it'.

'The camera!' Ken exclaimed. 'I must get that photo.'

'Yes. Quick, but not *too* quick. I mean, don't scare him.'

'No.' Ken quietly, carefully, picked up his camera from the stern, and set the flash-bulb mechanism. The Monster made no move. Ken raised the camera to his eye, and squinted through the view-finder.

'Dash it - I can't see a thing through this, in the dark!' he muttered, twisting the camera this way and that.

'Does it matter? Can't you sort of just aim it roughly in the right direction?'

'S'pose so. That's all I can do. I think I'd better

just risk it.'

'Oh, yes - do.'

Ken pressed the switch. There was a blinding blue-green flash, but only a little click for sound. A hundred lights seemed to dance before their eyes. Apart from these, neither of them could see a thing for seconds afterwards. There was no sound of splashing from the Monster.

Blinking, they rubbed their eyes, and peered. After a little they could make out Nestor still in the same position.

'Goodie!' Fiona cried, quite forgetting to whisper. 'You've not scared him, Ken. Take another while you've got the chance.'

'Sure.' The boy was already fumbling with the box containing the extra flash-bulbs. 'Just a minute. This takes time. Do you think we could get a slightly different view? Not quite so head-on? If you could use your oar-pull just a little to the left. Very gently. Yes.'

Fiona cautiously got her oar out, and dipped it into the water without any splashing. She began to pull the boat slowly round.

Ken's flash-bulb flared again, lighting up the night. Still Nestor remained apparently unmoved - though perhaps just a little lower in the water.

'Grand!' the boy said. 'That should be a good one. He's being jolly co-operative, isn't he?'

'Terribly. I'm sure he's a gentle creature, really,

for all his size. I'm getting quite fond of Nestor. He...'

She stopped abruptly. Behind them, from the shore, a broad white beam of light blazed out, illuminating them sharply in its glare - and equally illuminating the Monster.

Much shaken, the youngsters blinked into the brilliance, screwing up their eyes. Distinctly they could hear shouts from the shore. The searchlight beam swung away from them a little, to concentrate more fully on Nestor. Then, as suddenly as it had burst upon them, it was switched off. Dense blackness came down like a curtain.

'My aunt!' Ken panted. 'What a... what a... Mercy on us! Who... what on earth was that?'

'Goodness knows! It was terribly bright. What a glare! I can't see a thing. Those voices... somebody's been watching us; and now they've seen the Monster too.'

'Yes. Somehow they've stumbled on what we're doing. It's not our secret any more.'

'No. But at least we've got a photograph. Two of them. I hope, anyway. That's the main thing, isn't it?'

'Well... yes. So long as these wretched people don't beat us to it.'

'But they couldn't, could they? I mean - not yet? They can't have got a photo yet. Not at that distance?'

'They might with a telephoto lens. That light was probably bright enough to carry the distance. It wasn't any ordinary strong torch - it was some kind of searchlight. Probably a converted car headlight. The road is a long way back from there, so they must have brought this thing down to the loch specially. It would need a strong battery of some sort, or a portable generator. These are bulky things, which means that they were there specially to light up this bit of the loch - obviously to get a photograph of the Monster. This could not be a chance. It must have been organized...'

'Then... what are we to do, Ken?'

'We've got to do *something*, anyway - not just sit here. Look - I can see again, now. Nestor's gone.'

'So he has. That was a bit too much for him - and I don't blame him.'

'You know, Fiona, I think we ought to get ashore, and try to find out about these people: see who they are, and what they're up to, if we can. It's a pretty poor show if they're going to steal a march on us and get the photo and the £500 after we've done all the work, located Nestor's home area and found out how to bring him to the surface.'

'That's right. But what can we do?' asked Fiona.

We can row away northwards, round the headland again. If they can see us still, they'll think that we've just packed up. Then we can land at the other side of the point, and slip back along the shore. Look - don't you see a sort of glimmer of light amongst the trees, over there? No - further over.'

'Ye-e-es. Yes, there is something there.'

'It's about two-thirds of the way round this bay, and a bit back. Highish up, too - but of course the sides of the bay *are* high. Come on - oars out, Fiona!'

8
The Killers

THEY pulled away out of the bay, making no attempt to be silent, and round the headland of Rhubeg. At the far side of this they turned and rowed quickly in to the shore, which was here a shelving stony beach. The skiff was shallow and made landing easy. Hiding it under an overhanging alder tree, they took with them only the precious camera and Ken's pocket torch, and set off on foot, southwards again.

They crossed the headland and came to the broken ground above the bay, going very cautiously now, and as silently as possible. The hillside was fairly thickly wooded here, and though this gave them good cover it made the night seem darker, with roots to trip over and fallen twigs to crack. Fortunately the woods were of good Scots pines, and provided a soft carpet of pine needles instead of noisy dead leaves to walk over. They kept a hundred or so yards back from the shore, which here of course dropped steeply into the water. They could not see the glimmer of light that they had noted from the boat.

Leading the way, Ken crept on, making as nearly as he could for the place where he thought that the light had glimmered. They had to go slowly, for the ground was very rough, and it would have been easy to fall and make a noise. Every now and again they halted to listen. The night was quiet, except for the faint sigh of wavelets from the loch.

'I'm sure it was about here that the light was,' Ken whispered, presently. 'I wonder where they've gone?'

'I don't know. Maybe just back to the road? To a car?'

They moved on a little farther, and suddenly Fiona began to sniff.

'I can smell cigarette smoke,' she announced breathlessly. 'Can't you?'

'I believe I can. Yes - I've got it, too. Now - where is it coming from? There's no wind at all tonight.' Ken licked a thumb, and held it up, turning it about. It felt just slightly colder on the south-west side. 'What air there is comes from that direction.' He pointed. 'Further on, the way we've been going. Come on.'

They moved along, peering. At first they thought that they had lost the scent of the smoke, but in a little they got it again, more strongly. After about a hundred yards more they heard the low murmur of voices, still in front but down nearer to the water. Edging forward on tiptoe over the pine-needles, they crept downwards.

Quite a deep hollow amongst the trees opened suddenly before them, and at once the voices sounded more clearly. It was in deep shadow down there, and they could see nothing, save the red glowing of five cigarette-ends.

It was not difficult, on the still night air, to hear what was being said, and creeping as close as they dared, the young people listened.

One man, with a coarse Glasgow-sounding accent, was speaking. '...och, cut it oot, for Pete's sake!' he was saying strongly. 'I've got it a' worked oot. No use startin' too soon. We've got to let the folks get to their beds. We want folks asleep, see. We're goin' to make a lot o' noise, either way - rifle-fire or blastin'. We don't want folks bargin' along in a hurry to see where the noise is comin' from.'

'What aboot the wee man up in the croft? This Murdo?' another speaker asked. 'He's the nearest, is he no'?'

'I'm no' worryin' aboot him. He'll be right blotto by noo, him - wi' that bottle o' Scotch we gave him. Anyway, we can shut *his* mouth easy enough if he makes trouble. It's those kids, and their folks at the hotel. We've got to give them time to get to bed an' asleep, confound them!'

'Say, Mike - don't be too hard on the kids,' somebody else said, in a Cockney sort of voice this time. 'Where would we 'ave bin, without them kids? The old geyser Murdo gave us a lead on to the right place, but it was the kids as showed us how to get the crittur to come up, with lights on a rope.'

'Sure, Sammy. The kids had the right idea, granted. But if they heard *our* explosion, they'd likely jump to what we're doin' quicker'n other folk.'

'It ain't likely we'll have to blast the brute up, Mike. Likely it'll come up again with the light, an' we can shoot it.'

'Aye - but even a tommy-gun can make plenty of racket at night. We've got to have plenty time to make our getaway, boy. We've got a lot to do after the crittur's dead.'

Horrified, the listening youngsters stared at each other.

'I guess Mike's right.' This sounded like an American. 'We sure don't want nosy guys snooping around, till we've got the Monster safely towed up the lake.'

'I told you - I've got it all worked oot,' the man Mike interrupted. 'It's jist after ten noo. We'll wait another half-hour. Then Sammy an' Hank'll away doon for the drifter, an' sail it up here. Dead slow, so as to make no noise. They should be back by eleven-thirty. Ought to be late enough. Then we try this light racket, under the water, just as the kids did, an' when the crittur comes up we let it have it wi' the tommy-guns. We'll have to be real quick then, mind - or maybe the body'll sink. We'll have to get a couple o' ropes round it. If it sinks, *we're* sunk, an' bang goes ten-bloomin'-thousand quid!'

'Say - don't gimme the creeps, Mike!' the American pleaded. 'The body ain't gonna sink all that fast. Bodies never do. It better not, anyway! The Nebraska Museum of Science ain't offering thirty thousand bucks for a story - they want the body, the genuine hundred per cent Loch Ness Monster, dead or alive! We gotta get the body out of this lake all sound and shipshape.'

'Sure, Hank. Keep your hair on!' the man Mike cried. 'It's all taken care of, I tell you. All sewn up. We shoot it, and get ropes roond it quick. If it doesn't come up to the light, we let doon the gelignite, an' depth-charge it good an' strong. Enough to sink a bloomin' submarine! That'll either kill the crittur or stun it, an' it'll come floatin' up to the surface. We get the ropes on, an' tow it away. The barge is waitin' up at Lochend, at the head o' the loch an' the end o' the canal. Loadin' the thing into the barge'll take time, but yon crane will do the job fine. So long as we get that done, an' the pile o' logs back on top, before daylight, we're okay. Then we tow the barge through the canal to

Inverness in the mornin', open an' easy, an' oot to sea. Simple.'

'Yeah. It better be, Mister. We've sunk too much dough in this job to have any mistakes.'

A match struck to light a cigarette lit up also, for a moment, five men sitting down there in the hollow: five tough-seeming customers who looked like seamen.

One of them jerked a hoarse laugh.

'That brute is goin' to stink a bit, before we get it to the States!' he said.

'We've got that looked after, too,' Mike told him. 'We've got a pressure-spray, like you spray paint wi'. We spray it wi' the stuff they mothball the ships in. Like plastic. Keep it as good as new, or jist aboot. Nae bother - jist trust your Uncle Mike!'

'An' when do we get the dibs, Hank - the ten thousand smackers?'

'It'll be paid on delivery, Sonny. You ain't gotta worry about that. I guess that's the easiest part of it.'

Ken grasped Fiona's wrist. 'I say,' he whispered. 'The brutes - they're going to kill Nestor! *Kill* him! We've got to stop them.'

'Yes. Oh, we must! What can we do?'

'We'll have to get help, somehow, at once.'

'But how? Who can we get, at this time of night, in a place like this? And in time?'

'My father. We'll get Daddy. Maybe he'll think

of something.'

'Have we got time? To get to the hotel and back? He may be in bed by then.'

'No. I shouldn't think he'll go to bed till we're home. He'll wait up for us. We've got just over an hour. We'll have to hurry.'

'Yes. Come on, then.'

Quietly the pair of them crept back, until they were well clear of the hollow. Then, getting up, they tried to run. But the darkness under the trees was terribly confusing, and the roots and uneven ground played tricks with their feet. They kept tripping and stumbling and falling. In their impatience they seemed to go even more slowly than they had come. They had more than two miles to go.

'Look,' Ken gasped, after a while. 'We'd be better in the boat. Quicker. See where we're going, at least. This is hopeless. Be all night.'

'Yes. We can go straight... in the boat,' Fiona panted in reply.

So they turned down across the headland, still falling over things, and were thankful when they reached the waterside alders, found their boat, and tumbled in.

It was strange how much lighter the night seemed on the water, as they pulled away. With an oar each, they rowed their hardest. Ken's extra strength did no more than match Fiona's superior skill. They made the light boat fairly skip along - and certainly they got the impression of going much faster than their stumbling progress on land.

For all that it was nearly eleven before they reached the Ardroy jetty, and went running up the path to the hotel. Most of the lights in the house were out, but those of the lounge were still lit.

Major Rutherford must have heard them coming, and met them at the outer door. 'Well, I call this a pretty poor show!' he began, frowning. 'Your mother told you not to be late, Ken. She was beginning to be...'

'Daddy - you must come!' Ken broke in. 'Quickly. It's terribly important. Honestly.'

'Don't interrupt!' his father said, sternly. 'Your mother was getting anxious. I was just...'

'Listen, Daddy - please! You've *got* to!'

'You listen to *me*, instead, young man! When your mother and I tell you not to be late, we don't mean eleven o'clock...'

'Major Rutherford - we're terribly sorry for being late,' Fiona put in, breathlessly. 'But we couldn't help it. Some men are going to kill Nestor! The Monster!'

'Wha-a-a-at?' Major Rutherford blinked. 'Nestor? Monster? What on earth are you talking about? Are you both out of your minds?'

'No, Daddy - it's true. You must listen to me. We've found the Monster - oh, before tonight. We called it Nestor. Instead of Nessie, you know. But now some ghastly men are either going to shoot him, or depth-charge him. For £10,000. We've got to stop them.'

''Pon my soul, have you been reading horror comics, or something?' Ken's father demanded. 'Who's going crazy - you or me?'

'You, Daddy. I mean... not us, anyway! It's perfectly true. We couldn't tell you before, because... because... oh, well - leave that just now. The main thing is to get help, to stop these men - and quickly. We've only half an hour to get back.'

'Back where? What in the name of wonder are you babbling about, boy? £10,000! Nestor! Depth-charges! Are you trying to tell me that you imagine you've actually seen this mythical Monster?'

'Of course. It's not mythical. It's real - yards and yards of it. It sets up a wash a foot high. It...'

'Major Rutherford,' Fiona intervened again, as calmly as she could, gripping his sleeve. 'The Monster's *real*. We've got photographs of it in Ken's camera, but we can tell you all about that later. The thing is, we need help *now*. At once. Won't you believe me? Won't you come with us? Please!'

Ken's father drew a long breath. 'I... I... H'rrr'mph! Oh, well. Goodness knows what this is all about. We're undoubtedly all mad. Me too, to come with you, this time of night. But for your sake, Fiona...'

'Oh, good!' the girl cried. 'We can explain as we go, in the boat. Who else can we get? We'll need more help. There are five of these men...'

'Daddy was in the commandos. He's a match for three of them, at least,' Ken assured, confidently.

'Heavens above!' the Major gasped. 'Look here, I'm not going to get mixed up in any nonsense, now! Not on your young life, m'lad! I...'

'No, no,' Fiona said. 'I'm sure you won't actually have to fight.'

'I should jolly well think not!'

'But I do think we should be better with some reinforcements, just the same,' Ken went on. 'Has everybody else gone to bed?'

'Now, look here, young Ken, if you think I'm going to waken up inoffensive hotel guests and drag them out into the night on some wild goose chase like this, you're mistaken. I'll do no such thing.'

'A pity. We'll be terribly outnumbered, Daddy,' Ken said. 'The fishing ghillies would believe us, but they all live some way off. We haven't time...'

'Jakey,' Fiona suggested. 'What about Jakey?'

'Yes - Jakey. We could get him, at least. *He'd* come.'

'I dare say he would! That character strikes me as about as daft as the rest of you!' Major Rutherford declared.

'Come on, then, Dad.'

'Wait a minute! I'll have to go up and tell your

mother.'

'Oh, that'll take ages! And she'll not want you to go - any of us to go...'

'I... h'mmm... I won't tell her all this nonsense, of course. Never fear! I'll just say that you need my help - something to do with the boat. May be a little while, and not to bother staying awake.'

'Okay, Daddy - you do that. We'll go and get Jakey. He sleeps in an outhouse place at the back, but do be quick. Come right down to the jetty. Oh - and bring a torch.'

'Of all the crazy capers...!' Major Rutherford grumbled. The youngsters were no longer there to listen. Sighing, he turned and hurried upstairs.

9
Paying the Price

BY the time that a yawning and sleepy-eyed Jakey and the spluttering Major Rutherford had reached the little jetty, a new problem had arisen. Jakey's skiff was too small to take all four of them. They could all go in a larger boat, but that would mean getting the oars and rowlocks out of the boat-house, which was locked at night and the key kept in the hotel office. There was no doubt also that the larger boats were slower and heavier - and it was nearly eleven-fifteen already. Ken said that they just could not risk the delay.

Clearly there was nothing for it but to split up, one pair going in the small boat and the other coming along in a larger one just as quickly as possible. Since Ken and Fiona certainly were not going to separate at this stage, Jakey would just have to bring the Major along to the bay. Ken's father complained strongly that this meant that he still would not hear an explanation of what it all was about, but the young people declared that that would just have to wait. The main thing was speed!

Jumping into the skiff, Ken and Fiona pushed off, with Jakey already hurrying back to the hotel for the key to the boat-house, leaving poor Major Rutherford with all sorts of shouted instructions to do this and that and the next thing, but mainly to hurry after them to Rhubeg Bay just as fast as oars would row.

That long-suffering man stared after them helplessly.

Ken and Fiona broke all previous records in their race back to Rhubeg, yet they felt that they were just dragging along. They were still only halfway there when Ken's watch said eleven-thirty. They could only hope that the gang of men were delayed too.

At the headland they paused for a moment, breathless. 'Are we going to land, or stay in the boat?' Fiona panted.

'It's no good landing. I don't see what we could do on shore.'

'What are we going to do, on the water?'

'Can't say,' the boy admitted, 'But something, surely. We'll see what happens. At least we've heard no shooting, and no explosions. They can't have done anything yet. We'll move into the bay, shall we? Quietly.'

Keeping close in to the shore, they rowed carefully round the point. It did not take them long to discover what went on. A large boat lay in the middle of the bay, and from it a light was being lowered over the side. As this sank, another was coming up. The gang had at least two underwater lamps in action.

'Oh, I hope, I hope Nestor doesn't come up!' Fiona whispered.

'I don't know. It might be almost worse if they let off a big depth-charge of gelignite. They would probably kill him, and anything else that's down there too. They always might miss him with their tommy-guns. He's got a very small head.'

'I suppose so. But oh, what *can* we do? Do you think if we shouted?'

'They would never stop for *us*. If Daddy were here, they might pay some attention to a man's voice, but not to us. Remember, £10,000 is at stake.'

Anxiously they waited. The lamps rose up to the surface and disappeared below again and again. When they were up, their light showed the boat to have the lines of an ordinary sea-going fishing-drifter. Often these craft used the Caledonian Canal, and therefore Loch Ness, on their way from fishing grounds on one side of Scotland to the other. There would be nothing suspicious about this boat, once it was out in mid-loch again.

Suddenly a voice called from the shore. 'Ahoy - you blokes got the brute up yet? What a time you're takin'. You'd be better wi' the gelignite.'

'No' so much noise this way,' somebody answered him, from the boat. 'We'll try a bit longer. You'd better be ready wi' that blinkin' searchlight, Joe.'

'Aye, aye.'

'They've still got the searchlight on shore,' Ken said, low-voiced. 'That at least splits them up a little bit. Oh, I wish Dad and Jakey would hurry up!'

'They won't know what to do. I mean, they won't know where *we* are,' Fiona pointed out. 'They may land, even, at the point there. Don't you think we should go back, round the point, and signal them on? You still have your torch?'

'Yes. Maybe that would be best. I wish we could think of something.'

They rowed quickly back, under the shadow of the steep bank. They had only a short way to go round the headland again. They peered northwards, up the loch, but could see nothing.

'I think - yes, I think I hear the creak of rowlocks,' Fiona said. 'Listen.'

'Yes. I've got it. They're coming.'

'Flash your light, then.'

Ken switched his flash-lamp on and off a few times. There was no response.

'They'll have their backs to us, of course -

rowing. Keep doing it, Ken.'

Presently they were relieved to see a tiny answering gleam of light. It looked quite a long way off yet, but that was hard to calculate. Ken swung his own torch round in a few semi-circular waves, loch-wards, as a sign not to land. They hoped that the others would understand.

The young people turned back into the bay.

The lamp-raising and lowering was still going on. Voices in the drifter were sounding impatient. Ken kept the skiff under the cover of the headland's shore as much as he could. All that they could do was to wait.

Fiona was trembling with excitement, willing Nestor not to come up.

Of a sudden the skiff rocked, gently but quite noticeably. With quickly indrawn breaths the boy and girl gazed at each other. Then they peered about them anxiously.

They did not see it at first, for of course they were not in their usual place in the centre of the bay. Then they distinguished the long neck and small head just dimly in the gloom, out between them and the drifter but a little to the north.

'Oh, goodness!' Fiona exclaimed. 'He's come up! Now they'll shoot him. We must do *something*! Should we shout, make a noise? Maybe if we scared him?'

'They haven't spotted him yet,' the boy pointed

out. 'To shout would only draw attention to him, and it might not make him dive.' Ken bit his lip. 'Look - I think the only thing to do is to row out and try to get between the boat and Nestor - try and scare him into diving, and at the same time screen him from them. Keep them from shooting.'

'Yes. Yes - I was just going to say that. Oh, come on!'

'We shall have to be as quiet as we can. I hope they won't see us till the last moment. There's a risk, you know. I mean, to us. They may be pretty rough, these people...'

'We can't help that. They won't shoot *us*, at any rate. Quick, Ken! They may see him at any moment.'

Dipping in their oars, they urged the skiff out gently, without noise or splash, towards the middle of the bay. Nobody seemed to have noticed them as yet. It was very difficult to restrain themselves, to keep from plunging in their oars and rowing their hardest; but silence was now even more important than speed. The Monster remained motionless, watching.

As they drew nearer they could see that the people on the drifter all seemed to be leaning over the side, staring straight downwards. Evidently they expected the Monster to come up right at their lamps, directly alongside. It was just as well that they did, no doubt, or they surely would have noticed both the approaching skiff and Nestor himself. How much longer could this last?

It was when the smaller boat was no more than fifty yards from the drifter and a mere thirty from Nestor that they were spotted - and not from the boat at all but from the shore. A voice rang out.

'Hey - a bloomin' boat! Mike - d'you see it? Yon wee boat?'

'Whassat, Rab? Eh? Where?'

'Here, man. Gosh - it's thae kids again!' As he spoke the brilliant beam of the searchlight flashed out, white and strong. Dazzling, it caught the skiff fair and square.

'Say - see that!'

'Jings - the wee perishers!'

'Darn it - how'd they get there?'

A volley of shouts and angry cries echoed across the black water. Blinking and blinded in the blaze of light, the young people faltered in their rowing.

'I can't see a thing!' Fiona gasped. 'This is terrible!'

'It doesn't matter. So long as the light's on us, they probably won't see Nestor. But don't stop rowing. We're not properly between them and him, yet.'

'Clear oot, you kids!' someone shouted. 'Get oot o' this.'

'Yeah. Go on - scram!'

'Nosy wee brats! What d'you think you're doin'?'

'We've as much right to be here as you have!' That was Ken shouting back, in a brave effort to keep the men interested in them rather than in the Monster. Both the youngsters were rowing hard again.

'That's enough o' that!'

'No lip from you two - or you'll get thick ears!' they were told. 'Off wi' you!'

'No!' Ken cried. 'No!' They were coming nearly into a direct line between drifter and Monster now. That had its danger too, of course, for it meant that the men's glances would bear more and more in Nestor's direction. 'Shout. Say something, Fiona! Anything, to keep them looking at us,' the boy jerked.

They both began to yell defiantly, anything that came into their heads. It was too late. Another shout rose above their own.

'Jings - there it is! Look, there. The bloomin' Monster! There, behind them. It's up!'

'Gosh - so it is! Take a look at that, will you!'

'My goodness - what a crittur!'

'Quick - the guns! Don't stand starin', for Pete's sake!'

After that, everything happened with a rush. Yells from the drifter brought the searchlight swinging away from the skiff directly on to Nestor, who stared back into the glare as though mesmerized. Ken and Fiona worked their oars desperately in an effort to screen the Monster. Unfortunately the beast's head on its long neck rose higher out of the water than they did - and the drifter also was taller than they were, so that the men would still be able to see Nestor's head. Shouts to them to get out of the road followed thick and fast. Two men had short rifles in their hands - the Thompson sub-machine guns, no doubt.

'Get oot the way - or we'll shoot ower your heads!' they were warned. 'An' make it snappy!'

'Oh, why doesn't he dive?' Fiona burst out. 'With all this light and noise, you'd think he'd be scared!'

'Goodness knows! Listen - this is no use. They *could* shoot over our heads, and maybe hit him. Anyway, that's a motor-boat. They can move around far more quickly than we can. We shan't be able to keep this up much longer - to screen him. Look, we'll have to try and ram him!'

'What?'

'Yes, ram him. Try to make him dive. Scare him. Only thing we can do now.'

'But... oh, all right.'

Turning bows on to Nestor, they made a much smaller obstacle unfortunately; also, they swung a little way to one side. The enemy were quick to see this. There sounded behind them a savage rasping crackle, like the tearing of stiff strong canvas. Twice it barked out. The youngsters were aware of the swishing whine of shot somewhere to the right of them, and white water rose up in two lines of little spouts well behind Nestor and towards the land.

'Golly!' Ken almost choked. It was the first time that he had been under fire, but it sounded so like various films he had seen that he could not feel as afraid as he knew he should. He ducked, just the same. 'My goodness!'

Fiona was crouching almost double, too. 'Oh, Ken...!' she began, her lips trembling.

'Don't worry - they're not shooting at us,' the boy declared. That was to cheer himself up almost as much as his companion. 'Quick - don't stop pulling. We're too much to the left, as it is.'

Dreading another burst of fire, they rowed, if rather raggedly. Now they were back in their direct line, and the men would have to fire right above their heads to hit Nestor. This apparently they were not going to risk, at the moment, for it was another volley of shouts, not shots, that rang out.

There was one thing about the rifle-fire: it left the young folk fairly unconcerned about mere shouting. They pulled on, as fast as they could.

Glancing over his shoulder, Ken saw that they were not more than a dozen or so yards from Nestor. He was not looking at them, but gazing blankly into the glare of the searchlight, clearly quite dazed.

'Quick!' the boy panted. 'Only another few

yards. Be ready... he may upset us... as he dives. We're almost...'

He stopped at the sound that he least wanted to hear - the sudden throb of the drifter's powerful engine. This was the end, surely. The men could make rings round them, now - move swiftly into any position that they required to have a clear shot. The silly animal, absolutely fascinated by the light, paid no attention to this new noise either.

'It's no use!' Ken cried. 'They'll be round us, into range, any moment.' He drew in his oar, and turned round in the skiff. As he did so, a second blast of tommy-gun fire ripped out. It was another miss - but a much nearer one.

Ken searched for something to throw; they had no time now to try to ram. He grabbed the baling can, and hurled it directly at Nestor. But it was only a light tin, and did not carry half the length. Desperately he groped about for something else. There were only four other items in the boat: the underwater explosive charge, the electric torch, the camera, and the flashbulb mechanism. The charge was a heavy bulky thing, in its goldfish bowl. He would not be able to throw it for any length, but the splash might possibly alarm Nestor. Picking it up, he got to his feet, the better to throw it. The sudden movement set the light craft rocking, and the boy almost toppled overboard. His throw went wild, and the clumsy object fell into the loch with a big enough splash, but nowhere near Nestor, who paid no attention.

Out of the corner of his eye, Ken saw the drifter coming up fast on their left. He was aware of a great shouting going on, louder than before. He took up his torch - for the flash-bulb thing was too light to throw - and hurled it, hard. It was not a bad throw, but it missed Nestor by a foot, just the same. The animal only flicked its head.

'The camera!' Ken gasped. 'The... the camera? There's only that left?' It was a question that he was asking the girl, really.

'Oh, Ken!' she whispered, biting her lip.

'Look - there's Daddy! Just over there.' Ken pointed. Another boat, with Major Rutherford and Jakey each working an oar, was coming into line behind Nestor, but a good thirty yards back. That, no doubt, was why there had been a few moments' break in the shooting; the men could not fire without fear of hitting this new boat. No doubt too that was what all the extra shouting had been about. The drifter was circling round again to come in at another angle. The youngsters could distinctly hear one of the marksmen, the American, cursing over not getting a clear shot.

'Never mind, Hank - hold on!' the man Mike called out. 'You'll get him easy in a minute. The brute's sort o' hypnotized by the searchlight. Closer the better - an' easier to get the rope roond.'

Ken took up his camera. 'Will... will I?' he gulped.

'Yes,' Fiona said, decidedly. 'You must, Ken.'

They were now no more than eight or nine yards from the Monster. But the animal still was not looking at them, its head actually turned away from them, staring into the dazzle. The boy took a deep breath and careful aim, and hurled his precious camera from him with all his might.

The thing struck Nestor full and square on the head.

The result was as though they had touched off some sort of minor volcano. The Monster reared up and up out of the loch in sudden frenzy, long neck coiling, great massive body with its three humps for a moment largely clear of the surface, towering over the little boat, its long thick tail lashing the water into foam. Two flipper-like front feet pawed the air, and the little head jerked from side to side. It was a terrifying sight - but somehow the creature did not appear angry so much as frightened. Then, with an impact that showered splatters and spray all around, it crash-dived, and disappeared below in a tremendous flurry but at great speed. A vast wave rose up, and swept outwards.

The light skiff was overturned as though it had been a child's toy, and Ken and Fiona were flung violently into the water.

10
Goodbye, Nestor

DOWN and down the youngsters went. They felt as though they were being actually sucked down, as probably they were, by the pull of Nestor's dive. Panic clutched at them. Desperately they fought to struggle upwards, lashing out, trying to climb up in the black water.

It seemed an age before they felt the downwards drag slacken off, and they began to rise again. Even then their upwards progress seemed desperately slow. It appeared to be so much further to climb back. Their lungs were bursting, their ears ringing, and all sorts of lights were dancing in front of their eyes before at last they reached the surface and the blessed air. Side by side they bobbed up, gasping great mouthfuls of breath. It was brilliantly lit up here, compared with the blackness of those peat-stained waters.

For a few moments they were content to lie there

and gasp, treading water to keep themselves afloat. They were comforted to find themselves so close together. Then, as the panic died away, they began to look around.

This time, the skiff seemed to have sunk; at least there was no sign of it. But the drifter was fairly close at hand. Further away, on the other side, they could see that Major Rutherford's boat was still afloat and being rowed towards them with a deal of splashing. Nestor evidently had not come up again.

Though their ears were full of water and they could not hear very clearly, it was obvious that a great deal of angry and excited talk and shouting was going on aboard the fishing-boat. There seemed to be an argument in progress. Somebody was pointing down at them.

Ken shook his head, in an effort to clear the water out of his ears. He could hear better then.

'I'm tellin' you - it's oor only chance!' one man was crying. 'We canna come back - they'll have this place watched, noo. Put doon the gelignite, I say! Depth-charge the crittur!'

'No. We canna do that, man! We'd kill the kids!'

'Och, they'll no' be killed...'

'They would, I tell you! I've seen what depth-charges can do, afore this.'

'Well, haul the kids aboard us, then. Then the gelignite.'

'What would we do wi' them, after? We couldna

hold them - keep them quiet. We'd have the whole country after us! An' here's this other bloomin' boat, noo...'

'Reckon we should get the blazes outa here, Mike,' the American voice put in.

'Me, too, Mike! Jings - this is nae use...'

'Och, you're jist lily-livered scum! There's ten thousand quid doon there - an' a' we need to get it is a bit o' guts!'

'Shurrup, will you! D'you want to hang for your share o' the dough? I'm gettin' oot. We'll try another time, noo we know the place.'

'You got sump'n there, Mike. Let's get goin'.'

'You're yellow - that's what's wrong wi' the lot o' yous! Jist yellow!'

'Shurrup! Enough o' that sort o' talk. Stow it - or it'll be the worse for you! Come on - get that engine turnin'. Let's beat it.' The voice was raised still higher. 'Rab! Rab! Douse that light, an' scram. Aye - scram! We'll pick you up where we moored afore. Got it?'

Promptly the searchlight was switched off ashore, and at the same time the drifter's engine began to beat strongly. Soon the swimmers were bobbing about in a new wash, as the fishing-boat swung away and headed out into mid-loch.

Major Rutherford's boat bobbed too, for it was very close now, coming up as hard as oars could row.

'My goodness! You two all right?' Ken's father cried anxiously. 'Mercy on us - what a... what a business! I'd never have believed it! Look - catch hold of this oar, Fiona...'

Safely in the other boat, and shivering with both cold and reaction, the boy and the girl stuttered out bits of their story in fits and snatches. They could not tell all, there and then, naturally, but at least they did not have to convince Ken's father that they were not imagining it all.

'The trouble is, they'll come back,' Ken said, teeth chattering. 'Not tonight, maybe, but some other time. They'll do it again, and kill Nestor.'

'No, I think not,' his father declared. 'I'll notify the Fishery Board, and the police, and get this inlet, this bay, screened off somehow - guarded. Now we know that it is the Monster's home...'

'Nobody will believe you, Daddy! That's the whole trouble! People are so terribly obstinate and unbelieving? We... well, we know!'

'Oh. Ah... ummm! Well, of course, it is a little hard to take in, you know. I mean... Never mind - you've got these photographs you were talking about. That'll convince people.'

'But I *haven't*!' Ken's voice broke just a little. 'I haven't, any more.'

'He... he threw them away,' Fiona cried. 'He had to. He threw the camera at Nestor. With the spool inside!'

'What! You mean to say...?'

'Yes. It was the only way. It hit him - Nestor. I mean. That's why he dived. He would have been shot, otherwise. We had tried everything. Ken had thrown everything else...'

'This is extraordinary! You say that you've done all this, planned all this business, purely to win the £500 offered for a photograph of the Monster? And then, you just throw the photo away...!'

'Nestor's life is worth more than any £500, isn't it?' Ken demanded. 'We *had* to save him. It was all our fault, really - or at least, our responsibility. It was us who learned how to bring him up to the surface, by using a light. These men only copied us. It was up to us to save him, somehow.'

'I see. Yes, I understand. But... well, it must have taken some doing, young Ken! To throw it all away like that, I mean. You know, I think I'm rather proud of you!'

'It was Fiona told me I must do it. I don't think I could have done it otherwise.'

'Good girl, Fiona! I'm proud of you both, then.'

'Nothing to be proud about,' the boy mumbled, embarrassed. 'The thing is - how are we going to save Nestor another time? How are we to make people believe, so that we can get something done?'

'You maybe gave him such a fright, hitting him like that, that he will never come up to a light again?' Fiona suggested.

'Maybe. But I wouldn't like to rely on that.'

'I don't think that you need worry too much, Ken,' his father said. 'With four of us having seen it. We can all draw sketches of it. Couldn't we, Jakey?'

'Eh? Oh... well, aye.'

'Exactly. And I know the Fishery Board people pretty well. And the Chief Constable. I think I'll be believed, laddie. After all, I am... h'mm... a Justice of the Peace and, er, other things besides.'

His son swallowed, and Fiona tried to look suitably impressed.

'Oh, well...'

'Yes. So don't you worry about our Nestor.' That 'our' was just slightly stressed. 'Just leave it all to me.'

Ken winked at Fiona, but probably she did not see him in the dark.

'Now, time I got you safely back to the hotel, before you both catch pneumonia, and before anybody back there takes hysterics! It must be midnight, at least. Time you were all in bed. High time.'

'Yes, Daddy.'

'Of course, Major Rutherford,' added Fiona.

'Ooh, aye.'

'What are you grinning at, the two of you?'

'Nothing, Daddy - nothing at all.'

As the rowers dug in the oars, Fiona leaned over the side. 'Goodbye, Nestor,' she whispered. 'Forgive us - we didn't mean you any harm.'

11
In the News

IT was almost a fortnight later when the Postie brought Fiona MacBride another letter, back in her own island of Eorsa. It was not a very long letter, in the same handwriting as the last one, and it read like this:

Dear Fiona,

I thought you would be interested in this newspaper cutting. It's from the 'News Dispatch' of yesterday.

Hope you had a good journey home. We had - though it was rotten having to leave Loch Ness.

See you soon again, I hope. I wonder what sort of scrape we'll get into next time?

Yours ever,

KEN

P.S. I'm going in to Edinburgh tomorrow to see about that cine-camera.

P.P.S. Daddy's sent a cheque to the Ardroy Lodge Hotel to buy a new skiff for Jakey.

P.P.P.S. I hope you can cope with this bit of paper. A promise is a promise.

P.P.P.P.S. Aren't newspaper people awful in the things they say! Jolly decent, too, though.

The piece of newspaper enclosed bore large and striking headlines.

LOCH NESS MONSTER SENSATION

BOY AND GIRL FOIL MURDEROUS ATTACK

NEWS DISPATCH ACCLAIMS HEROES

It can now be revealed - and the *News Dispatch* is proud to be the only newspaper to publish this exclusive story - that not only has the Loch Ness Monster been seen again, and photographed and its home bay discovered, but the animal has been the object of a dastardly attack by shooting, and only the heroism and initiative of a young Scots boy and girl saved its life.

The boy and girl, who do not wish their names to be made public, went to Loch Ness

News Dispatch

in an effort to take a photograph of the Monster to win the £500 prize offered by this newspaper. By methods which the authorities wish not to be disclosed at present, these young people traced the Monster's home area to a certain bay, and managed to get two flashlight photographs of the creature by night; one of a small head, long neck, and three humps, and another of head and neck only.

Unfortunately a gang of unscrupulous men, attracted by reports of the Monster having been seen by crofter Murdo Macleod, were watching this district, with a view to killing the animal and selling the carcase to an American museum which was offering £10,000 for the Monster, dead or alive. (It will be recalled that Mr Bertram Mills, of the circus, offered £20,000 for the creature, but alive, some years ago.) This gang saw the young people at their night-time photography, in a boat, and moved in to shoot the animal. In their spirited efforts to save the creature, the boy and girl did everything in their power to make it dive, and ended by throwing even their camera containing the spool with the two photographs in it, directly at the Monster, hitting it on the head. All this took place while automatic fire was going on. They managed to save the Monster, but lost camera and photographs in the process.

The *News Dispatch* is satisfied that this

News Dispatch

account is true. It is substantiated by reliable eye-witnesses, whose sketches of the Monster are printed below. In appreciation of the young people's initiative, self-sacrifice and courage, this newspaper has sent to the boy's father a cheque for £250, being half the sum offered for the photograph, as compensation and encouragement, to purchase new cameras, possibly. The Editor and proprietors wish them every success in the future.

The *News Dispatch* is glad to be able to report that the Monster's life is now safe from any further attempts illegally to kill it, at least in its home bay. The fishery authorities and the police have erected a boom, or water-barrier, across the mouth of the bay that will prevent any craft from entering it, and the steep sides of the bay itself will prevent any boat from being launched into it from the land.

For the preservation of a unique survival from another age, all Britain has to be grateful to two brave and determined young people.

Underneath was a selection of the drawings that they had made of Nestor, at Major Rutherford's suggestion - and Fiona giggled at the sight of them in print. Ken's effort was fairly realistic; his father's was more like a worm crawling out of the earth than anything else; Jakey's was quite unrecognizable and probably had been printed upside-down; while her own looked like nothing so much as a cross between a camel and a giraffe, most surprised.

The girl stopped giggling, however, as she turned the newspaper cutting over. Pinned on the back was a cheque, made out to Miss Fiona MacBride, for £100 sterling.

In Preparation

Spaniards' Isle

by

NIGEL TRANTER

'The beam from the torch shone on something else. Ken gulped, gasped, almost choked behind his mask. The eel had been bad enough, but this was terrifying...'

A sunken Spanish Galleon lay just beneath the waves off a small island in the Hebrides – was it full of treasure? No one except Fiona believed that Ken had really seen the galleon from the aeroplane, but with the help of a young fisherman, and some borrowed diving gear, they were soon exploring the secrets of the wreck – and experiencing its dangers.

Will Ken and Fiona find the treasure? And if they do, will they be able to stop it falling into the hands of the poachers who are hiding on the island?

ISBN 0 9515151 9 5